SECRET LIVES, HIDDEN TRUTHS

ONESIMUS MALATJI

Secret Lives, Hidden Truths
By: Onesimus Malatji

Third-Party Content:

This book may reference or include content from third-party sources. The author and publisher do not endorse or take responsibility for the accuracy or content of such third-party material.

Endorsements:

Any endorsement, testimonial, or representation contained in this book reflects the author's personal views and opinions. It does not imply an endorsement by any third party.
Results Disclaimer: The success stories and examples mentioned in this book are not guarantees of individual success. Actual results may vary based on various factors, including effort and circumstances.

Results Disclaimer:

The success stories and examples mentioned in this book are not guarantees of individual success. Actual results may vary based on various factors, including effort and circumstances.
No Guarantee of Outcome: The strategies, techniques, and advice provided in this book are based on the author's experiences and research. However, there is no guarantee that following these strategies will lead to a specific outcome or result.

Fair Use Notice:

This book may contain copyrighted material used for educational and illustrative purposes. Such material is used under the "fair use" provisions of copyright law.

DEDICATION

Being one of the difficulties in my family, always stubborn, I thank God I turned out alright. I dedicate this book to my mother, Esther Malatji. I will always love you. You have raised me well until I became a fully grown man. Thank you for your prayers and support during my tough times in life. Additionally, I extend my heartfelt dedication to my beautiful wife, the partner of my life, Petunia. You have been there for me and our family, and you are truly one in a million – the best motivator. I thank God for having you as my spouse, partner, and my inspiration; you are one of my most special and wonderful gifts. During times of trials, you have never walked out on us. Thank you. I love you so much.

I also send this dedication to my brother Edward "Gong," one of the greatest creative businesspersons alive. Thank you for being a wonderful brother and supporting me in times of need and trial. May God bless you and increase your business anointing. I love you so much. Special greetings to my sister Bertha, your passion for food will undoubtedly touch the world. I love you.

Furthermore, I extend my love and dedication to my brother Mohau; I will always cherish you, brother. Special Dedication for Galetsang & Dineo I will always love you no matter what. This is also for my friends, and fellow soldiers in war: Zama, Panana, Tshwane, Blessing, Lowen, Winners I love you guys – you are my family. Special Gratitude to my inspirer my mother. I deeply respect the gift that God has put in you, and I am immensely grateful for having you while I was putting this book together.
Thank you, my dear mother, Esther Malatji. I love you so much

ACKNOWLEDGMENTS

I extend my deepest gratitude to everyone who has been a part of this incredible journey, both seen and unseen. Your support, encouragement, and unwavering belief in me have been the driving force behind the creation of this book.

To my family, for standing by me through thick and thin, for believing in my dreams, and for being a constant source of inspiration – your love and encouragement have been my guiding light.

To my friends, mentors, and colleagues, your valuable insights and feedback have shaped the ideas within these pages. Your willingness to share your wisdom and experiences has enriched this work beyond measure.

To all those who have supported me on my path, whether through a kind word, a helping hand, or a moment of shared understanding, thank you. Your presence in my life has made all the difference.

To the countless individuals who have faced challenges and setbacks, yet continued to strive for greatness, your stories have fuelled the inspiration behind these words. May you find solace and encouragement within these pages.

And finally, to the readers who have embarked on this journey with me, thank you for allowing me to share my thoughts and experiences. It is my hope that this book serves as a beacon of hope, a source of guidance, and a reminder that fulfilment can be found in every step of life's intricate tapestry.

With heartfelt appreciation,

Onesimus Malatji

SECRET LIVES, HIDDEN TRUTHS

1. Crossed Paths 11-12
2. Unspoken Bonds 13-15
3. Shadows of the Past 16-18
4. Flamboyant Facades 19-20
5. Secret Lives, Hidden Truths 21-22
6. A Dangerous Legacy 23-24
7. Whispers of the Heart 25-27
8. The Enemy Within 28-30
9. Forbidden Desires 31-33
10. A Tangled Web 34-36
11. Echoes of Betrayal 37-39
12. Under the Cloak of Night 40-41
13. Unravelling Secrets 42-43
14. Consequences Unfold 44-45
15. Broken Vows 46-47
16. The Weight of Guilt 48-50
17. Colliding Worlds 51-53
18. Legacy of Loss 54-56
19. Reckoning of the Heart 57-58
20. A Family Divided 59-60
21. Chains of the Past 61-62
22. Unveiling the Mask 63-64
23. Edge of the Abyss 65-66
24. Shattered Illusions 67-68
25. The Gathering Storm 69-70
26. Revelations Unearthed 71-72
27. Bloodlines Entwined 73-75
28. Faces of the Enemy 76-78
29. A Truth Too Heavy 79-80
30. Epilogue: Silence of the Fallen 81-82
31. Afterword 83-84

SECRET LIVES, HIDDEN TRUTHS

PROLOGUE

In the heart of the city, under the shroud of twilight, two worlds were about to collide in a way that would change everything. This is a story of love and betrayal, of secrets buried deep within the folds of family legacies. It is a tale that weaves through the lives of Mark, a man haunted by his father's shadow, and Selina, a woman ensnared in the web of her family's dark past.

As the city lights flickered to life, casting long shadows across the streets, Mark stood at his window, looking out at the sprawling metropolis. His life, a tapestry of success and respectability, was about to unravel in ways he could never have imagined. The secrets he had fought so hard to keep buried were clawing their way to the surface, threatening to consume everything he held dear.

Not far away, Selina moved through her elegant home, each step a reminder of the world she had tried to leave behind. Her life, filled with luxury and appearances, belied the turmoil that simmered just beneath the surface. The legacy of her family, notorious in the underworld, was a shadow that followed her every move, a ghost from which she could not escape.

Their paths, marked by the choices of their pasts, were on the brink of intersecting. A chance encounter, a moment of shared understanding, would set them on a journey fraught with moral dilemmas and emotional turmoil.

This story is not just about the choices we make, but also about the ones made for us, the ones that shape our lives in ways we cannot foresee. It is about the chains of the past and the possibility of breaking free, about finding light in the darkest of places.

As you turn these pages, prepare to enter a world where the boundaries between right and wrong are blurred, where love and betrayal dance closely, and where secrets have the power to heal or to destroy.

CROSSED PATH

The evening air was crisp, the kind that hinted at the approach of autumn but still clung to the last whispers of summer. In the heart of the city, nestled among sprawling gardens, an elegant affair was underway. The sounds of refined chatter and soft music floated on the breeze, mingling with the rustling leaves of ancient oaks.

Mark stood at the edge of this scene, a glass of expensive champagne in his hand. He was a man who looked like he belonged in such settings, with his sharp suit and confident posture. Yet, there was a hint of discomfort in his eyes, a subtle out-of-placeness that he masked well. Across the garden, Selina moved among the guests, her laughter light and her demeanour graceful. Dressed in a gown that shimmered under the soft lighting, she was a vision of elegance. But like Mark, her smile didn't quite reach her eyes. There was something else there, a depth of something unsaid, a story untold.

Their paths crossed near a secluded part of the garden. Mark had stepped away for a moment of solitude, and Selina had wandered off, perhaps in search of the same. Their eyes met, and there was a moment of silent acknowledgment, a recognition of something familiar in the other. "Quite the event, isn't it?" Mark finally said, his voice breaking the silence between them. "It is. But sometimes, I find the most interesting stories are not in the crowd but in the quiet corners," Selina responded, her gaze still holding his.

They talked then, their conversation flowing more easily than either would have expected. Mark spoke of his work in the financial sector, carefully curating his words to avoid any mention of the darker chapters of his life. Selina talked of her interests, of art and literature, but steered clear of the shadows that lurked in her own history. As the night wore on, it became clear that there was an understanding between them, a shared sense of something more beneath the surface. They were two people, each carrying their own secrets, their own burdens, yet finding an unexpected solace in the company of the other.

The evening came to an end, and they parted ways, a lingering look shared between them. It was a look that spoke of a mutual curiosity, a desire to delve deeper into this unexpected connection. Mark returned to his wife, Lerato, who waited with a knowing smile, unaware of the shift that had just occurred in her husband's world. Selina re-joined her husband, his arm slipping comfortably around her waist, the picture of marital contentment. But as they left the garden and the night closed in, both Mark and Selina were left with the echoing sense of something profound just beginning. It was a feeling that neither could shake off, a sense that their paths crossing that night was not just a mere coincidence, but the start of something much more significant.

UNSPOKEN BONDS

The morning after the event, the memories of the previous evening lingered in Mark and Selina's minds. There was a sense of something unexplained, a connection that seemed to transcend their respective realities. Mark found himself at his desk, staring unseeingly at the reports in front of him. His thoughts were elsewhere, replaying his conversation with Selina. He was drawn to her, not just by her physical beauty, but by the shared understanding that seemed to pass between them. The feeling unsettled him; he was a married man, after all. Yet, he couldn't deny the intrigue she sparked in him.

Elsewhere, Selina sat in the quiet of her luxurious home, her husband already off to work. She thought about Mark, about the ease with which they had conversed. There was a comfort in speaking with someone who seemed to understand the unvoiced struggles, the weight of living a life that wasn't quite truthful. It was a rare connection, and it intrigued her.

Days later, a chance meeting brought them together again. This time it was at an art exhibition, a neutral ground far removed from the grandeur of the garden party. Their eyes met across the room, and there was an instant recognition, a conscious acknowledgment of the connection they had felt.

They walked together, commenting on the artwork, but the conversation quickly turned personal. Selina spoke of her life, of the pressures of maintaining appearances, the charade of perfection. Mark shared his own experiences, the constant balancing act between who he was and who he needed to be.

In these moments, they found an understanding in each other that they hadn't found with their spouses. It was an unspoken bond, forged not just by mutual attraction but by the shared experience of living a life that wasn't entirely their own.

As they parted ways that day, there was a silent agreement between them. An acknowledgement that what they were embarking on was complicated, possibly even dangerous, but undeniably compelling. It was more than just an emotional affair; it was a connection that touched on something deeper, something more profound.

Mark returned to his life, to his wife, but the encounter left him restless. Selina, too, found herself distracted, her thoughts constantly drifting to Mark. They were both aware of the lines they were toeing, the risks involved in pursuing this connection.

But as "Unspoken Bonds" draws to a close, it was clear that whatever was unfolding between them was only just beginning.

There was an undercurrent of something inevitable, a path that they were both helplessly being drawn down. It was a path fraught with potential heartache and complications, but one that they seemed unable to resist. "Unspoken Bonds" deepens the intrigue and complexity of Mark and Selina's relationship, setting the stage for the emotional and moral dilemmas they will face as their story unfolds.

SHADOWS OF THE PAST

"Shadows of the Past" delves deeper into the backgrounds of Mark and Selina, exploring how their hidden histories shape their present and influence their growing connection. The city was just beginning to wake, its streets bathed in the soft light of dawn. Mark, however, had been awake for hours, his mind a whirlpool of thoughts. In a decision driven by a mix of nostalgia and restlessness, he found himself driving through the neighbourhood of his youth. The buildings, now more rundown than he remembered, stood as silent witnesses to his turbulent childhood.

Each corner of the street, each graffiti-covered wall, brought back memories of a life he had long tried to leave behind. He remembered the sound of his father's voice, a blend of harshness and affection, teaching him the ways of the street. These memories were in stark contrast to the life he had meticulously built, a life of respectability and success.

Selina, on the other hand, was in her father's mansion, a sprawling estate that felt more like a fortress. As she sat across from her father at breakfast, she was reminded of the dual nature of her life. Her father, a man of power and danger, had always provided for her, yet the source of their wealth was a constant shadow hanging over her seemingly perfect life.

The chapter then follows Mark and Selina through their day, their interactions with family and colleagues punctuated by flashbacks to their pasts. Mark's visit to his old neighbourhood ends with a chance encounter with someone from his father's past, a reminder that no matter how far he's come, his past is never too far behind.

For Selina, a phone call from an old family acquaintance brings her face to face with the realities of her father's empire. The call, innocuous on the surface, hints at the ongoing activities of her father's business, activities she has tried to distance herself from.

As the day ends, Mark and Selina reflect on their pasts and the lives they have built. For Mark, the visit to his old neighbourhood leaves him feeling unsettled, a reminder of a world he's tried to forget. Selina, after the phone call, feels the weight of her family legacy more acutely than ever.

The chapter concludes with Mark and Selina meeting again, this time by chance on a busy city street. The brief encounter is charged with an unspoken understanding of the burdens they carry. They part with a look that speaks volumes, a recognition of the shadows that haunt them both.

"Shadows of the Past" reveals the depth of Mark and Selina's characters, exploring the impact of their family legacies on their present lives. It sets the stage for the unfolding drama, hinting at the challenges they will face as they navigate their connection against the backdrop of their complicated pasts.

FLAMBOYANT FACADES

"Flamboyant Facades" explores the stark contrast between the public personas of Mark and Selina and their inner realities, as they navigate the complexities of their lives and their growing connection. In the heart of the city, under the dazzling lights of a grand ballroom, the elite gathered for another evening of opulence and masked pretences. Among them were Mark and Selina, each playing their part to perfection in this well-choreographed social dance.

Mark, accompanied by Lerato, mingled with the crowd, his smile practiced and his conversation polished. To the outside world, he was a man who had it all - success, charm, a beautiful wife. Yet, within him, there was a growing sense of dissonance, a feeling of being trapped in a life that felt increasingly like a well-crafted lie.

Selina, radiant in her elegant dress, laughed and conversed with an ease that belied her inner turmoil. By her husband's side, she was the picture of grace and contentment. But beneath the surface, her mind was elsewhere, troubled by the reality of her existence, a life built on foundations she wished she could escape.

As the night progressed, Mark and Selina found themselves together on a balcony, away from the prying eyes of the social elite. Here, the façades they maintained slipped, and they found themselves sharing a moment of honesty.

They spoke of the weariness of living lives that felt more like performances, of the exhaustion that came with maintaining the flamboyant facades. In this shared vulnerability, their bond deepened, a connection formed not just through mutual attraction but through an understanding of each other's hidden struggles.

The chapter juxtaposes the glittering world of the event with the internal conflicts of the protagonists. Mark's interactions with business associates and Lerato are interspersed with his internal struggle to reconcile his past with his present. Similarly, Selina's engagement with the guests and her husband masks her internal conflict about her family's illicit legacy and her place in it.

As the evening comes to an end, Mark and Selina return to their respective spouses, the masks firmly back in place. The ride home for both is reflective, as they ponder the dualities of their lives and the authenticity of their relationships.

Lying in bed, they both stare into the darkness, contemplating the complexities of their lives. The chapter closes with them each pondering the growing connection between them - a relationship that seems to be the only genuine thing in their lives of pretence. "Flamboyant Facades" explores the theme of duality, contrasting the external appearances with the internal realities of Mark and Selina. It sets the stage for future conflicts as they continue to navigate their complicated lives and the undeniable bond they share.

SECRET LIVES, HIDDEN TRUTHS

Secret Lives, Hidden Truths," delves deeper into the dual lives of Mark and Selina, exploring the stark contrast between their public personas and their concealed, true selves. In the world of high finance and social prestige, Mark navigated his day with practiced ease. At a high-end business meeting, he was the picture of professionalism, discussing complex deals with a confident air. Yet beneath this polished exterior, Mark was wrestling with inner demons. His mind often drifted to the starkly different world of his childhood, marked by crime and danger, a world he feared might one day catch up to him.

Meanwhile, Selina, adorned in her philanthropic role, attended a charity gala. With a radiant smile and engaging conversation, she charmed the attendees, discussing the importance of giving back. But this facade hid her inner conflict. The wealth she so generously gave away was tainted, a product of her father's notorious legacy in the drug world. She felt like a fraud, using the spoils of her father's empire to cleanse her guilt.

As Mark and Selina each navigated their respective worlds, they were acutely aware of the masks they wore. Their public images were carefully curated, a far cry from the realities they concealed. They were prisoners of their pasts, trapped in lives built on half-truths and deceptions.

Their paths crossed again in a clandestine meeting at a secluded café, away from the eyes of their usual circles. In this haven, they shed their facades and shared their fears and frustrations. Mark opened up about his constant battle to keep his past hidden, while Selina shared her guilt and the hypocrisy of her life.

Their conversation turned to their families, and for the first time, they unveiled the full extent of their hidden truths. Mark confessed about his father's criminal activities, revealing the dark underbelly of his childhood. Selina, in turn, shared the burdens of being a drug lord's daughter, the heavy legacy she carried.

This exchange marked a turning point in their relationship. Their bond deepened, anchored in a mutual understanding of living lives shrouded in secrets. They found in each other a rare comfort, a space where they could be their true selves, unburdened by the weight of their facades.

As they parted ways, the reality of their situations settled in. They were each entangled in a web of lies, a precarious balancing act that threatened to unravel at any moment. The chapter closed with them returning to their lives, their minds heavy with the complexities of their secret lives and the undeniable connection they shared. "Secret Lives, Hidden Truths" exposes the inner turmoil and conflicts of Mark and Selina, setting the stage for the dramatic developments to come in their intertwined stories. It underscores the theme of the past's inescapable influence on the present and the perilous nature of hidden truths.

A DANGEROUS LEGACY

We show the deep and perilous histories of Mark and Selina's families, revealing how these legacies continue to impact their lives and the choices they face. As the city dawned a new day, Mark found himself in his father's old study, a room he seldom entered. Surrounded by remnants of a life once lived in the shadows of the law, he felt the weight of his heritage. Old photographs, newspaper clippings, and mementos of a criminal empire stared back at him, a stark reminder of the legacy he had been desperately trying to outrun.

Meanwhile, Selina faced her own legacy in a more direct confrontation. She visited her father, who was growing frail but still held a tight grip on his empire. Their conversation, laced with tension and unspoken accusations, revolved around the future of the family business. Her father's expectation for her to continue his legacy clashed with her desire for a life untainted by crime.

The chapter then intertwines the personal struggles of Mark and Selina with their growing relationship. They meet secretly, finding solace in each other's company. As they share their fears about their family legacies, they realize the danger that lurks beneath their connection. Their families, steeped in crime and rivalry, could pose a real threat if their relationship were to be discovered.

In a series of flashbacks, the chapter reveals key moments from their pasts. For Mark, it's a recollection of a violent episode that marked the end of his involvement in his father's world. For Selina, it's the memory of a harrowing night that made her vow to never be a part of her father's dealings.

Their current lives, though seemingly detached from their pasts, are still influenced by these legacies. Mark's business dealings are occasionally questioned for integrity, a reflection of his father's reputation. Selina's philanthropic work is often shadowed by whispers about the source of her wealth.

The chapter ends with a pivotal moment. As Mark and Selina part from another secret meeting, they are unaware that they have been observed. This realization sets off a chain of events that begins to unravel the carefully constructed worlds they live in.

"A Dangerous Legacy" reveals the depth of the struggles Mark and Selina face, not just in their personal lives but also in the broader context of their family histories. It highlights the complexities of trying to escape a past that is deeply intertwined with their identities and sets the stage for the escalating challenges they will face as their story unfolds.

WHISPERS OF THE HEART

"Whispers of the Heart," focuses on the internal emotions and growing intimacy between Mark and Selina, as they navigate the complexities of their connection amidst their challenging personal lives. In the quiet hours of the early morning, Mark lay awake, his wife's steady breathing a contrast to the turmoil in his mind. His thoughts were a tangled web, with images of Selina weaving through them. There was an undeniable pull towards her, a connection that went beyond mere physical attraction. It was as if she spoke directly to the hidden parts of his soul, parts he had long since buried.

Selina, in her own home, experienced similar restlessness. The memory of her last meeting with Mark lingered in her mind, their conversation echoing in her heart. She was drawn to the honesty and vulnerability he showed, qualities she found lacking in her own marriage. In Mark, she saw a reflection of her own struggles, a shared longing for something more authentic.

The chapter delves into the growing emotional intimacy between Mark and Selina. Their secret meetings become more frequent, each encounter deepening their understanding of each other. They share their hopes, fears, and dreams, conversations filled with a raw honesty that neither had experienced with their spouses.

As they continue to navigate their respective lives, the contrast between their public personas and their private selves becomes more pronounced. Mark finds himself increasingly distant from Lerato, their conversations superficial and strained. Selina's interactions with her husband are similarly hollow, their marriage a façade maintained for appearances.

The chapter also explores the internal conflicts Mark and Selina face. Mark struggles with guilt over his growing emotional infidelity, while Selina grapples with the fear of stepping out of the only life she's known. They both understand the potential consequences of their actions, yet find themselves unable to resist the pull towards each other.

In a pivotal moment, Mark and Selina acknowledge their feelings, though they do not yet act on them physically. This acknowledgement brings a sense of relief mixed with apprehension. They know their connection could shatter the lives they've built, yet the authenticity of their emotions is something neither can deny.

"Whispers of the Heart" concludes with Mark and Selina parting from another clandestine meeting, their hearts heavy with unspoken words and unacknowledged desires. The chapter leaves the reader with a sense of anticipation about how they will handle this deepening bond amidst the complexities of their respective lives.

This captures the emotional depth of Mark and Selina's relationship, highlighting the internal battles they face as they are drawn closer to each other. It sets a tone of longing and introspection, adding layers to their characters and the choices they must make.

THE ENEMY WITHIN

The narrative by focusing on the internal and external conflicts faced by Mark and Selina, as their relationship evolves amidst the backdrop of their complicated personal lives and hidden pasts. The city's skyline was bathed in the golden hues of dusk as Mark sat in his study, a sense of unease gnawing at him. The recent closeness he shared with Selina brought not only comfort but also a heightened awareness of the internal conflict he had been battling for years. His past, a world he had tried so hard to leave behind, seemed to be encroaching upon his present, fuelled by the connection he had with Selina, a woman with a similarly troubled legacy.

Selina, in her elegantly appointed home, faced her own turmoil. Her marriage, once a haven, now felt more like a prison. The conversations with her husband, once filled with shared plans and laughter, had become mere formalities. The realization that she was more connected to Mark, a man she had only recently met, than to the man she had shared years of her life with, was both shocking and telling.

As their secret meetings continued, both Mark and Selina began to confront the enemies within themselves – their unfulfilled desires, the secrets they harboured, and the moral dilemmas their relationship posed. They were both married, and the knowledge that they were treading into forbidden territory weighed heavily on them.

In a particularly poignant moment, Mark confessed to Selina the depth of his internal struggle. He shared his fears of becoming like his father, of the darkness he felt lurking within himself, a darkness he feared might one day consume him. Selina listened, her own heart heavy with the knowledge of her family's criminal activities, understanding all too well the fear of being tainted by one's bloodline.

The chapter also sheds light on the growing suspicions of their spouses. Lerato, observant and intuitive, began to notice the subtle changes in Mark – his distant gazes, the unexplained absences. Similarly, Selina's husband started to question the changes in her behaviour, her distractedness, and her sudden absences.

Towards the end of the chapter, a twist unfolds as Mark accidentally discovers a connection between his and Selina's families – a revelation that hints at a deeper, more dangerous link than either of them had anticipated. This discovery sends shockwaves through Mark, leaving him to grapple with the implications of their relationship and the hidden ties that bound their families.

"The Enemy Within" concludes with Mark and Selina meeting in the wake of this discovery, their conversation filled with tension and uncertainty.

The chapter leaves the reader on a cliff-hanger, wondering how this revelation will impact their relationship and what choices they will make in the face of this new reality. This explores the theme of internal conflict and the impact of past legacies on present choices. It heightens the narrative tension, revealing more complexities in Mark and Selina's relationship and setting the stage for future developments in their story.

FORBIDDEN DESIRES

The escalating emotional and physical tension between Mark and Selina, as they grapple with the intensifying connection between them and the moral implications of their growing desires. The city was cloaked in a velvety night as Mark and Selina found themselves in the secluded confines of a dimly lit restaurant. The ambiance around them was intimate, a stark contrast to the turmoil raging within them. Their meetings had become more frequent, and with each encounter, the line they were treading grew increasingly blurred.

This night, their conversation was laced with an undercurrent of unspoken emotions and suppressed desires. They spoke of mundane things, but their eyes, their gestures, spoke of a deeper, more primal communication. The air between them was charged with an electric tension, a palpable desire that they had both been trying to ignore.

Mark, tormented by the feelings he harboured for Selina, was also acutely aware of his commitment to Lerato. The guilt he felt was overwhelming, yet he found himself unable to stay away from Selina. His life with Lerato, once a source of happiness, now felt like a distant memory, overshadowed by the intense connection he shared with Selina.

Selina, equally conflicted, found herself torn between the safety of her marriage and the exhilarating yet dangerous liaison with Mark. Her relationship with her husband, once comfortable and secure, now felt suffocating, a stark reminder of the life she was living, a life that felt more like a well-rehearsed play than reality.

As the evening progressed, their conversation became more daring, more suggestive. The attraction between them was undeniable, and the more they tried to resist, the stronger it seemed to grow. It was a dance of temptation, each step bringing them closer to the edge of a precipice they both knew could lead to their downfall.

In a moment of weakness, a moment where desire overpowered reason, their conversation ceased, and they found themselves locked in a passionate embrace. It was a kiss that sealed their fate, a physical manifestation of the emotional turmoil they had been experiencing.

The chapter concludes with them parting ways, the reality of what had transpired hanging heavily over them. They were both aware of the consequences of their actions, the potential destruction of their marriages, and the scandal that would ensue if their affair were to be discovered.

"Forbidden Desires" leaves the reader at a crucial juncture in the story, where Mark and Selina must confront the reality of their actions and the impact it could have on their lives and the lives of those around them. This captures the pivotal moment in Mark and Selina's relationship, exploring the themes of temptation, betrayal, and the consequences of forbidden love. It sets the stage for the complex emotional and moral dilemmas they will face in the aftermath of their actions.

A TANGLED WEB

The complexities and repercussions of Mark and Selina's affair, exploring how their actions begin to affect not only their lives but also those around them, weaving a web of deception and consequences. In the aftermath of their passionate encounter, Mark and Selina found themselves ensnared in a web of their own making. The reality of their situation became more apparent with each passing day. Their secret meetings, once a source of solace, now carried a weight of guilt and apprehension.

Mark, returning home to Lerato, felt the burden of his betrayal. Every smile, every touch from his wife, was a reminder of the duplicity of his actions. He began to withdraw, his responses becoming more mechanical, his mind constantly replaying the moments spent with Selina. The distance between him and Lerato grew, the once warm and loving atmosphere of their home turning cold and strained.

Selina, on the other hand, faced a similar struggle. Her husband's presence, once comforting, now felt like a constraint. She moved through her days in a daze, her interactions with him perfunctory, her thoughts always returning to Mark. The guilt of her infidelity weighed heavily on her, creating a chasm in her marriage that seemed to widen with each passing day.

As the chapter unfolds, the narrative shifts to Lerato and Selina's husband, both of whom begin to sense the changes in their spouses. Lerato, intuitive and sensitive, noticed Mark's increasing detachment, his distracted demeanour. She began to question the foundation of their marriage, her suspicions growing with each unexplained absence.

Selina's husband, observant in his own right, also started to perceive the cracks in their relationship. His inquiries about her day, her whereabouts, became more frequent, his gaze holding a hint of suspicion that was hard to miss.

The web of lies and deceit began to take its toll on both marriages. Mark and Selina found themselves caught in a vortex of their own emotions, torn between their obligations and the undeniable connection they shared. In a dramatic twist, a chance discovery by Lerato sets the stage for a confrontation.

She stumbled upon a piece of evidence that hinted at Mark's infidelity, a revelation that threatened to shatter the façade of their perfect life. The chapter ends with Mark and Selina each facing the looming threat of their secret being exposed. The tangled web they had woven was beginning to unravel, the consequences of their actions looming over them like a dark cloud.

"A Tangled Web" heightens the tension and drama in the narrative, exploring the impact of Mark and Selina's affair on their marriages and setting the stage for the impending conflicts and revelations. It captures the emotional turmoil and complexity of navigating the consequences of forbidden desires.

ECHOES OF BETRAYAL

The emotional fallout and escalating tension following the revelation of Mark and Selina's affair. This chapter explores the repercussions of their actions, the sense of betrayal felt by their spouses, and the internal conflicts faced by Mark and Selina as they grapple with the consequences of their decisions. In the cold light of day, the reality of their situation settled heavily on Mark and Selina. The discovery of their affair sent shockwaves through their lives, unravelling the fabric of their marriages and exposing the lies they had so carefully constructed.

Lerato, having confronted Mark with the evidence of his infidelity, was a maelstrom of emotions. The man she thought she knew, the life they had built together, now seemed like a farce. Her feelings oscillated between anger, hurt, and disbelief. Mark's attempts at explanation, his pleas for understanding, fell on deaf ears. The trust they had shared was shattered, leaving behind a chasm filled with pain and betrayal.

Similarly, Selina's husband, confronted with the undeniable truth, struggled to come to terms with the revelation. His reaction was one of stunned silence, the kind that spoke volumes. The questions he had, the doubts he harboured, all were confirmed in the most painful way. Selina's apologies, her tearful admissions, did little to bridge the gap that had formed between them.

As the chapter progresses, Mark and Selina find themselves isolated in their respective worlds, each dealing with the fallout of their actions. Their secret meetings, once a source of comfort and connection, now seemed like a distant memory, tainted by the reality of their betrayal.

The narrative delves into the emotional turmoil experienced by both characters. Mark, ridden with guilt, struggled to come to terms with the pain he had caused Lerato. He grappled with the realization that his actions had destroyed the very foundation of his marriage. Selina, equally remorseful, faced the disintegration of her marriage, her life as she knew it crumbling around her.

The chapter also explores the impact of the affair on Lerato and Selina's husband. They each deal with their sense of betrayal in their own way, their emotions a complex web of hurt, anger, and disillusionment. The life they had known, the partners they had trusted, had changed irrevocably.

"Echoes of Betrayal" concludes with Mark and Selina each facing the harsh consequences of their actions. They are left to navigate the ruins of their relationships, the echoes of their betrayal reverberating through their lives.

The chapter ends on a note of uncertainty, leaving the reader wondering what the future holds for these intertwined lives. This captures the emotional depth and complexity of the aftermath of an affair, highlighting the pain and consequences faced by all involved. It sets a sombre tone for the narrative, exploring the themes of trust, betrayal, and the difficult path to redemption.

UNDER THE CLOAK OF NIGHT

"Under the Cloak of Night," intensifies the narrative by delving into the aftermath of the exposed affair and the covert actions taken by Mark and Selina as they attempt to navigate the shattered pieces of their lives. The city was shrouded in darkness, the streets quiet except for the occasional whisper of night wind. In this cover of night, Mark found himself driving aimlessly, the events of the past few days replaying in his mind. The confrontation with Lerato, her tears and anger, had left him feeling hollow. His home, once a sanctuary, now felt like a prison of his own making.

Similarly, Selina wandered through her expansive garden, the moon casting long shadows on the path. The tension in her house was palpable, her husband's silent treatment a constant reminder of the betrayal. Their home, once filled with laughter and warmth, now echoed with the silence of a love lost.

As the night deepened, Mark and Selina, driven by a need to escape their respective realities, found themselves at their usual meeting spot, a secluded park bench overlooking the city. The urgency of their situation, the gravity of their choices, was lost in the momentary comfort they found in each other's presence.

Their conversation was a mix of regret, longing, and a desperate search for solace. Mark spoke of his guilt, the pain of hurting Lerato, and the uncertainty of his future. Selina shared her own turmoil, the coldness in her home, and the realization that her marriage might be beyond repair.

In the quiet of the night, they discussed their options, the possibility of leaving everything behind and starting anew. But the reality of such a decision, the impact on their families and the lives they had built, weighed heavily on them.

The chapter also sheds light on Lerato and Selina's husband, both of whom are grappling with their own pain and decisions. Lerato, feeling betrayed and alone, seeks comfort in a friend, pouring out her heartache and confusion. Selina's husband, on the other hand, finds himself in a bar, his silent brooding interrupted by an unexpected encounter that offers a new perspective on the situation.

"Under the Cloak of Night" concludes with Mark and Selina parting ways, the uncertainty of their future looming large. They return to their homes, to the lives they have disrupted, each step heavier than the last. This explores the themes of regret, longing, and the consequences of decisions made in the heat of passion. It captures the emotional turmoil of Mark and Selina, as well as the ripple effects of their affair on their spouses, setting the stage for further developments in this tangled narrative.

UNRAVELLING SECRETS

"Unravelling Secrets," delves into the revelations and discoveries that begin to surface, further complicating the lives of Mark, Selina, and their spouses. This chapter explores the unfolding of hidden truths and the impact these revelations have on each character. As dawn broke over the city, the light seemed to pierce through the shadows of deception that had enveloped Mark and Selina's lives. The chapter begins with Lerato, who, in her quest for understanding and closure, stumbles upon a series of emails and messages that unravel more secrets about Mark's past. She discovers connections to his father's criminal world that Mark had never disclosed, deepening her sense of betrayal and confusion.

Meanwhile, Selina's husband, fuelled by a mixture of anger and a need for answers, starts his own investigation into Selina's past. His probing leads him to unearth details about her family's criminal activities, information that Selina had always kept hidden from him. This revelation forces him to reassess not only their marriage but also his own values and beliefs.

As the narrative progresses, Mark and Selina grapple with the consequences of their actions, now compounded by the emerging truths about their pasts.

Mark faces a confrontation with Lerato, where he is forced to explain not just his affair with Selina, but also the hidden aspects of his life connected to his father. This confrontation is charged with emotion, revealing the deep cracks in their relationship.

Selina, on the other hand, has a painful discussion with her husband. The exposure of her family's history and her own complicity in hiding it shakes the foundation of their relationship. The trust and understanding they once shared are now overshadowed by feelings of deception and disillusionment.

The chapter also explores the internal conflicts of Mark and Selina as they come to terms with the unravelling of their secrets. The realization that their affair has set off a chain reaction of revelations and pain leads them to question not just their decisions, but also the very foundations of their identities.

This concludes with Mark and Selina meeting in the aftermath of these revelations, their relationship now mired in a complex web of truth and consequences. They stand at a crossroads, unsure of how to move forward, both in their relationship with each other and with their spouses. This chapter deepens the narrative, highlighting the impact of hidden truths coming to light and the emotional turmoil that ensues. It sets a tone of introspection and consequence, driving the story towards a climax where each character must confront the reality of their actions and decisions.

CONSEQUENCES UNFOLD

"Consequences Unfold," addresses the aftermath of the unravelling secrets, focusing on how the characters deal with the repercussions of their actions and the changes in their relationships.

In the wake of their exposed secrets and the affair, Mark and Selina, along with their spouses, confront the stark reality of their situations. The chapter opens with Mark, who faces the immediate consequences of his actions. His relationship with Lerato reaches a breaking point as she grapples with the double betrayal – his affair and his hidden past. The pain and disappointment in Lerato's eyes are palpable, and their once loving home turns into a battleground of hurt feelings and broken trust.

Selina's life, too, is in turmoil. The revelation of her family's criminal background and her affair with Mark causes a deep rift with her husband. The trust and foundation of their marriage crumble under the weight of her deceptions. Their interactions are fraught with tension and recriminations, the emotional distance between them growing with each passing day.

As the chapter progresses, Mark and Selina find themselves increasingly isolated. Mark's sense of guilt and regret over hurting Lerato consumes him. He begins to question the choices that led him to this point, reflecting on the potential costs of his actions on his personal and professional life. Selina, faced with the coldness of her husband and the disintegration of her marriage, feels a profound sense of loss. The life she had known, the identity she had crafted, all seem to be slipping away. She is left to confront the reality of her choices and the uncertain future that lies ahead.

The chapter also delves into the emotional journey of Lerato and Selina's husband. Lerato, struggling to come to terms with the betrayal, seeks solace in friends and family, trying to find a way forward. Selina's husband, on the other hand, grapples with a mix of anger and disillusionment, his perception of Selina irrevocably altered.

"Consequences Unfold" concludes with Mark and Selina facing the harsh reality of their actions. Their affair, once a secret escape from their respective lives, has led to a cascade of revelations and consequences that extend far beyond their own personal guilt and regret. The chapter ends on a note of uncertainty, with each character standing at a crossroads, forced to confront the ramifications of their choices. This is a crucial turning point in the narrative, highlighting the theme of consequences and the ripple effect of decisions made in secrecy. It sets the stage for further developments and the choices that the characters must make in the wake of the upheaval in their lives.

BROKEN VOWS

"Broken Vows," delves into the emotional aftermath and decisive actions taken by the characters as they confront the reality of their broken marriages and the irrevocable changes in their lives.

The chapter opens with Mark and Lerato in a tense and heart-wrenching confrontation. The air between them is thick with unsaid words and unshed tears. Lerato, once the pillar of strength and understanding in their relationship, now looks at Mark with a blend of sorrow and indignation. The revelation of Mark's affair and his hidden past has shattered her trust, leaving her to question the very foundation of their marriage. The discussion culminates in Lerato's decision to separate, a painful but necessary step to protect her own emotional well-being.

Simultaneously, Selina's marriage faces a similar fate. Her husband, unable to reconcile the woman he loved with the secrets she kept, decides that their marriage cannot continue. Their conversation is one of finality, with Selina's apologies and explanations falling on deaf ears. The chapter portrays Selina's profound sense of loss, not just of her marriage, but of her identity and the life she had built.

Mark and Selina grapple with the reality of their broken vows. Mark is wracked with guilt, his actions having cost him the love and trust of his wife. He reflects on his journey, how his affair with Selina, initially an escape, has led him to this juncture of loss and regret. He starts to face the consequences not only in his personal life but also in his professional sphere, as whispers of his personal turmoil begin to affect his work.

For Selina, the end of her marriage brings a different kind of introspection. The freedom she thought she desired now feels hollow and isolating. She is confronted with the realization that her choices have led to irrevocable changes, not just in her relationship with her husband but also in how she views herself.

The chapter also touches on Lerato and Selina's husband as they start to rebuild their lives, navigating the pain and betrayal. They find themselves on unexpected paths, seeking new beginnings and grappling with the reality of moving on from relationships they once thought unbreakable.

"Broken Vows" closes with Mark and Selina finding solace in each other, yet both are aware that their relationship has come at a high cost. They stand together, yet apart, united by their shared experiences but divided by the guilt and repercussions of their actions. This marks a pivotal point in the narrative, emphasizing the theme of consequences and the emotional turmoil of broken relationships. It sets a sober tone for the story as it explores the complexities of starting over and the lingering impact of past choices on the future.

THE WEIGHT OF GUILT

"The Weight of Guilt," go deeply into the emotional burdens and introspection experienced by Mark and Selina, as they come to terms with the consequences of their actions and the impact those actions have had on those they love. In the quiet aftermath of their shattered relationships, Mark and Selina find themselves wrestling with an overwhelming sense of guilt. The chapter opens with Mark in his now almost empty house, the absence of Lerato's presence making the space feel cavernous and cold. He is haunted by memories of their life together, each corner of the house a reminder of what he has lost. His thoughts are a maelstrom of regret, self-reproach, and a deep-seated realization of the pain he has caused.

Selina, similarly, faces the stark reality of her actions. The luxury of her home, once a symbol of success and happiness, now feels like a gilded cage, echoing with the loss of her marriage. She is consumed by thoughts of her husband, the life they built together, and the irreversible damage her deception has wrought.

As the chapter progresses, both characters struggle to navigate their daily lives under the heavy burden of their guilt. Mark's performance at work suffers, his usual focus and drive diminished by his internal turmoil. Colleagues and friends notice the change, but Mark remains isolated, trapped in his own cycle of remorse.

Selina, too, finds little solace in her usual activities. Her social engagements, once a source of pleasure, now feel hollow and meaningless. She withdraws from her circle of friends, her mind preoccupied with the fallout of her choices.

The narrative also explores the deeper impact of their guilt on their sense of self. Mark begins to question the man he has become, the values he has compromised, and the path that led him to this point. He grapples with the realization that his actions have not only broken his marriage but have also fundamentally altered his own identity.

For Selina, the guilt is compounded by the knowledge of her family's criminal past, a legacy she had tried to distance herself from, but which now seems inextricably linked to her current predicament. She reflects on her life choices, the lies she has lived, and the person she wants to be.

The chapter closes with a poignant scene where Mark and Selina meet, their conversation a mix of empathy and shared pain. They support each other, yet there is an understanding that their relationship is the root of their current suffering. The chapter ends with them both looking out into the city, a physical representation of their internal isolation and the complex journey ahead.

"The Weight of Guilt" is a deeply introspective chapter, focusing on the emotional aftermath of betrayal and the long road to forgiveness and self-redemption. It sets a reflective and sober tone for the story, underscoring the theme of personal responsibility and the challenging path to finding inner peace.

COLLIDING WORLDS

"Colliding Worlds," the seventeenth chapter of your book, escalates the narrative by bringing the separate worlds of Mark and Selina, as well as their spouses, into a complex and dramatic convergence. This chapter explores the intersections of their lives and the unexpected consequences that arise from their affair. As the consequences of their actions continue to ripple through their lives, Mark and Selina find their separate worlds colliding in unforeseen ways. The chapter begins with a seemingly unrelated event – a social gathering where both Lerato and Selina's husband are present. The interaction between them, initially casual, takes a turn as they slowly realize the common thread that connects them: their spouses' affair.

Meanwhile, Mark, grappling with his own turmoil, makes a decision to confront his past more directly. He visits his father, a man he has long distanced himself from, seeking answers and perhaps a form of closure. This confrontation is emotionally charged, revealing layers of family history and unresolved tension.

Selina, in an attempt to find her own peace, visits a place from her childhood, a location that holds significant memories related to her family's criminal activities. Her journey is introspective, filled with reflections on her choices and the impact of her family's legacy on her life.

The chapter takes a dramatic turn when Mark, following his visit with his father, finds himself inadvertently crossing paths with Lerato and Selina's husband at the social gathering. The encounter is tense, filled with unspoken emotions and questions. Mark is confronted with the pain and anger in Lerato's eyes, a stark reminder of the hurt he has caused.

Simultaneously, Selina, returning from her introspective journey, learns about the encounter and rushes to the scene, fearing the potential fallout. Her arrival adds to the already charged atmosphere, creating a scene where all the primary characters are present, each dealing with their own emotions and revelations.

As the chapter progresses, truths are spoken, accusations made, and emotions laid bare. The confrontation serves as a catharsis for some, while for others, it deepens the wounds. The interactions between the characters are complex, reflecting the tangled web of relationships and betrayals.

"Colliding Worlds" concludes with a sense of unresolved tension. The characters leave the gathering, each lost in their thoughts, reflecting on the revelations and confrontations. The chapter ends with a sense of uncertainty about the future of these intertwined lives.

This chapter heightens by bringing together the various threads of the story in a dramatic and emotionally charged setting. It explores the themes of confrontation, revelation, and the complex nature of human relationships, setting the stage for future developments in the story.

LEGACY OF LOSS

"Legacy of Loss," goes into the deep emotional impact and the sense of loss experienced by the characters as they come to terms with the consequences of their actions and the irreversible changes in their lives. In the aftermath of the dramatic confrontation, Mark, Selina, Lerato, and Selina's husband each confront the magnitude of their loss. The chapter opens with Mark in a state of introspection, reflecting on the legacy of loss he has inherited from his father and perpetuated through his own actions. He realizes that the cycle of betrayal and pain he has continued not only affects his personal life but also casts a long shadow over his sense of self.

Selina, grappling with the consequences of her actions, confronts the loss of her marriage and the disillusionment of her ideals. The realization that her actions have contributed to the perpetuation of her family's legacy of deceit and pain weighs heavily on her. She struggles with the understanding that her choices have irrevocably altered the course of her life and the lives of those she cared about.

Lerato, in the wake of her separation from Mark, faces the loss of the life and future she had envisioned. She finds herself re-evaluating her past, questioning the decisions that led her to this point, and trying to reconcile the image of the man she loved with the reality of his actions.

Selina's husband, too, deals with a profound sense of loss. The discovery of Selina's affair and her family's criminal background shatters his understanding of their relationship. He struggles with feelings of betrayal and the loss of trust, which form the cornerstone of any relationship.

As the chapter unfolds, the narrative explores the parallel journeys of these characters as they navigate their individual paths of grief and acceptance. Mark and Selina, now separated from their spouses, face the loneliness and guilt that come with their choices. They each embark on a journey of self-discovery, attempting to understand their motivations and seeking redemption for their past actions.

The chapter also touches upon the theme of how the past shapes the present. Mark and Selina's reflections reveal how their family legacies influenced their choices and contributed to the current state of their lives. It is a legacy marked by loss – loss of trust, loss of relationships, and loss of the life they once knew.

"Legacy of Loss" concludes with a poignant scene where Mark and Selina, now aware of the full extent of the damage caused by their affair, meet to discuss their future. The chapter ends on an uncertain note, with both characters standing at a crossroads, unsure of the path ahead but aware that their decisions will have lasting implications.

This goes deep into the emotional aftermath of the characters' actions, exploring themes of loss, introspection, and the quest for redemption. It sets a contemplative for the story, underscoring the complex nature of personal choices and their far-reaching consequences.

RECKONING OF THE HEART

"Reckoning of the Heart," explores the emotional and moral reckoning faced by Mark and Selina as they confront the deepest aspects of their feelings, motivations, and the consequences of their actions. This chapter is pivotal in their journey towards understanding, acceptance, and the potential for redemption.

In the quietude that follows the storm of their exposed affair, Mark and Selina grapple with the depths of their emotions and the reality of their choices. The chapter begins with Mark in solitude, reflecting on the journey that led him to this point. He ponders over the reckoning of his heart – the battle between love and duty, desire and responsibility. The quiet of his now empty home echoes the emptiness he feels inside, a stark reminder of the cost of his choices.

Selina, in a similar vein, faces her own reckoning. She reflects on the cascading effects of her actions, not just on her marriage, but on her sense of self. She confronts the hard truths about her motivations for the affair – the escape it provided from her own unhappiness and the allure of a connection that seemed to understand her innermost self.

As the narrative unfolds, both characters delve into a deep introspection. Mark questions the nature of love and loyalty, pondering whether the feelings he harboured for Selina were born out of true connection or a desire to escape his own hidden demons.

Selina meanwhile, contemplates the notion of freedom and the price she has paid for it – the loss of her marriage and the disruption of the life she knew.

The chapter also explores the concept of forgiveness – both seeking it from those they've hurt and granting it to themselves. Mark and Selina each face the daunting task of forgiving themselves for their actions, a necessary step in their journey towards healing and moving forward.

"Reckoning of the Heart" reaches its climax in a poignant encounter between Mark and Selina. In this meeting, they share their individual reflections and realizations. The conversation is laden with emotion – a mix of regret, understanding, and a faint glimmer of hope. They acknowledge the deep connection they share but also recognize the pain and disruption their relationship has caused.

The chapter concludes with both characters at a crossroads. They stand on the brink of deciding what the future holds for them – whether to continue down the path they have started together or to part ways in an attempt to mend the lives and relationships they have damaged. "Reckoning of the Heart" goes into the emotional and moral complexities of Mark and Selina's relationship. It highlights the theme of introspection and the difficult process of coming to terms with one's actions and their repercussions. This chapter sets the tone for the forthcoming decisions and paths that Mark and Selina will choose in the subsequent chapters of the story.

A FAMILY DIVIDED

"A Family Divided," delves into the broader impact of Mark and Selina's affair, highlighting the division and strife it causes within their families. This chapter explores the strained relationships and the emotional toll on family members, widening the lens to show the ripple effects of their actions.

In the wake of the tumultuous events, the chapter begins with Lerato, who is trying to come to terms with the crumbling of her marriage. She finds herself in a whirlwind of emotions, grappling with feelings of betrayal and the challenge of explaining the situation to family and friends. Her family, once close-knit and supportive, is now divided, with some members expressing anger and disappointment towards Mark, while others urge her to consider reconciliation.

Similarly, Selina's husband, now estranged, struggles with his own family's reaction to the revelation of the affair and the criminal background of Selina's family. His family, who had welcomed Selina as one of their own, feels betrayed and deceived. The chapter portrays their confusion and hurt, as they try to reconcile the image of the woman, they knew with the secrets that have come to light.

As the narrative progresses, the impact on Mark and Selina's extended family is further explored. Mark's visit to his father, hoping for some form of understanding or support, ends in disappointment. His father, still entrenched in his own criminal past, is unable to offer the empathy or guidance Mark seeks. This encounter leaves Mark feeling more isolated, highlighting the division within his own family.

For Selina, the strain extends to her relationship with her siblings, who are divided in their reactions to her affair and the revelations about their father's past. Some express sympathy for her situation, while others are critical, viewing her actions as a betrayal of family values. The chapter also touches upon the emotional impact on the children in the families. Although not directly involved, they sense the tension and the changes in family dynamics, adding another layer of complexity to the situation.

"A Family Divided" concludes with Mark and Selina separately reflecting on the wider consequences of their affair. They come to realize that their actions have not only affected their spouses but have also caused deep divisions within their families, leading to strained relationships and a sense of alienation. This expands the scope of the narrative to include the familial impact of the affair, exploring themes of betrayal, division, and the search for understanding within a family context. It sets a poignant and reflective tone, highlighting the far-reaching consequences of personal decisions on family dynamics and relationships.

CHAINS OF THE PAST

"Chains of the Past," explores how the histories and backgrounds of Mark and Selina continue to influence and entangle their present lives, acting as chains that constrain their choices and actions. In this chapter, both Mark and Selina are forced to confront the inescapable nature of their pasts and how these histories have shaped their current predicaments. The narrative opens with Mark revisiting places from his childhood, each location a tangible reminder of his father's criminal legacy. He realizes that no matter how far he has come, the shadows of his past continue to loom over him, influencing his decisions and relationships.

Selina, on the other hand, finds herself delving into old family records, uncovering more about her father's illicit activities. She discovers secrets and truths she had been shielded from, understanding more deeply how her life has been shaped by her family's choices. This exploration is a painful acknowledgment of how the past continues to hold a grip on her life.

As the chapter progresses, the narrative delves into the psychological impact of their family legacies on Mark and Selina. Mark struggles with feelings of predestination, wondering if he was ever truly free to make his own choices, or if his path was always going to be influenced by his father's deeds. Selina grapples with a similar dilemma, questioning whether her actions were ever truly her own or merely a reaction to the legacy she was born into.

The chapter also explores the theme of breaking free from the past. Mark and Selina each seek ways to distance themselves from their family histories, looking for paths that might lead them to a future unburdened by their legacies. This search is fraught with challenges, as both find that escaping the chains of the past is not a simple task.

Interwoven with Mark and Selina's personal struggles are glimpses into the lives of Lerato and Selina's husband. Lerato begins to seek closure, exploring ways to move beyond the betrayal and rebuild her life. Selina's husband, meanwhile, finds himself reflecting on his own family's history, recognizing that everyone has elements of their past they wish to escape.

"Chains of the Past" concludes with Mark and Selina meeting to discuss their discoveries and reflections. They share a moment of mutual understanding, recognizing that while their pasts may shape them, they also have the power to forge new paths for themselves. This chapter underscores the theme of the enduring impact of one's past and the struggle for personal liberation from historical and familial legacies. It sets a tone of introspection and determination, as the characters seek to understand and potentially free themselves from the chains of their histories.

UNVEILING THE MASK

"Unveiling the Mask," focuses on the revealing of true identities and intentions, as the characters confront the realities behind the facades they have maintained. This chapter is pivotal in stripping away the illusions and pretences, leading to a deeper understanding of themselves and each other. The chapter opens with Mark in a moment of profound self-reflection. He recognizes the facade he has maintained for so long – the successful businessman, the devoted husband, the man who has escaped his father's shadow. Confronted with the collapse of his marriage and the consequences of his affair, Mark begins to question who he truly is beneath all these masks. His journey leads him to confront uncomfortable truths about his desires, his fears, and his motivations.

Similarly, Selina faces her own moment of unveiling. For years, she has played the role of the perfect wife and philanthropist, all the while hiding her family's dark past and her own dissatisfaction with her life. The unravelling of her marriage forces her to confront the reality of her situation – she has been living a life that was more about appearance than genuine fulfilment.

The narrative then shifts to a poignant encounter between Mark and Selina. This meeting is different from their previous ones; there is an air of raw honesty as they both drop their facades. They talk openly about their fears, their regrets, and the longing for a life that is true to

who they are. It's a cathartic moment for both, as they see each other –
and themselves – more clearly than ever before.

Lerato and Selina's husband, meanwhile, embark on their own journeys
of self-discovery. Lerato starts to peel back the layers of her identity
that had been defined by her marriage to Mark. She begins to
rediscover her individuality, her strengths, and her aspirations beyond
the role of a wife. Selina's husband confronts the illusions he had about
his marriage and his wife. His journey is one of re-evaluation, as he
grapples with feelings of betrayal and the task of redefining his life
moving forward.

"Unveiling the Mask" concludes with Mark and Selina acknowledging
that their affair, though born out of mutual understanding and
connection, was also an escape from facing their individual truths.
They stand at a crossroads, aware that the path forward requires them
to embrace their authentic selves, no matter how daunting that may be.
This is crucial in the narrative arc, highlighting the theme of self-
realization and the importance of living authentically. It sets the stage
for the characters' future decisions and the potential for personal
growth and transformation.

EDGE OF THE ABYSS

"Edge of the Abyss," captures a crucial turning point in the narrative. It brings the characters to a critical juncture where they face the profound consequences of their actions and stand on the precipice of significant life changes. In this chapter, both Mark and Selina find themselves metaphorically at the edge of an abyss, looking into the depths of the chaos their actions have created. The gravity of their situation and the uncertainty about the future weigh heavily on them.

For Mark, this realization hits hard as he faces the prospect of a divorce and the disintegration of the life he once knew. He grapples with deep feelings of remorse and loss, not just for his marriage but for the trust and love he once shared with Lerato. Mark's professional life also starts to feel the strain, as rumours of his personal troubles begin to affect his business relationships and reputation.

Selina, dealing with her own set of challenges, confronts the reality of her broken marriage and the disillusionment of her dreams. The life of privilege and security she had known with her husband now seems like a distant memory. She faces the daunting prospect of starting over, of building a new life on the ruins of the old.

The chapter also delves into the emotional turmoil of Lerato and Selina's husband. Lerato finds herself battling a mix of sadness and liberation, torn between her love for Mark and the pain he has caused her. Selina's husband, meanwhile, faces his own abyss, as he tries to come to terms with the end of his marriage and the revelations about Selina's past.

In a moment of reflection, Mark and Selina meet to discuss their uncertain futures. Their conversation is tinged with a sense of desperation and fear. They acknowledge the depth of the abyss they are facing – the potential loss of everything they hold dear. This meeting is not just about their relationship but also about confronting the reality of their situations.

"Edge of the Abyss" concludes with both Mark and Selina making crucial decisions about their next steps. They realize that whatever choices they make, there will be significant consequences – not just for themselves, but for everyone involved in their lives. This chapter poignantly captures the theme of facing the consequences of one's actions and the difficult journey towards redemption and rebuilding. It sets a tone of uncertainty and introspection, paving the way for the characters' eventual decisions and the paths they choose to take in the face of their personal crises.

SHATTERED ILLUSIONS

"Shattered Illusions," deals with the painful process of confronting and accepting the harsh realities that shatter the illusions each character held about their lives, relationships, and themselves. The chapter opens with Mark, alone in his office late at night, surrounded by the trappings of his success yet feeling utterly hollow inside. He reflects on how his affair with Selina and the subsequent fallout have shattered his illusion of having a perfect life and marriage. He realizes that his pursuit of happiness was based on a foundation of lies and escapism, not just in his marriage but also in the persona he created to distance himself from his father's criminal legacy.

Selina, in her now quiet and empty home, grapples with the realization that the life she had built with her husband was more about maintaining appearances than genuine contentment. The unravelling of her marriage forces her to confront the uncomfortable truth that her happiness had been built on a façade, and she had been complicit in its maintenance.

Lerato, reeling from the shock of Mark's infidelity, comes to terms with the reality that her marriage was not as secure and honest as she had believed. She starts to see Mark in a new light, understanding that there were aspects of his life and character she had been blind to. This revelation is painful, but it also gives her the clarity to start thinking about her own needs and future.

Selina's husband, too, faces his own shattered illusions. He must come to grips with the fact that the woman he loved and trusted was not who he thought she was. This realization is a bitter pill to swallow, and it challenges his perceptions of trust and loyalty in relationships.

As the chapter progresses, Mark and Selina confront the ruins of their respective marriages and the personal myths they had created about their lives. They both face the difficult task of re-evaluating their choices and the people they have become. This process is fraught with emotional turmoil but also offers a glimmer of hope for personal growth and honesty.

"Shattered Illusions" culminates in a scene where Mark and Selina meet, not as lovers, but as two individuals seeking understanding and redemption. Their conversation is raw and honest, devoid of the pretences that had once defined their relationship. They acknowledge the pain they have caused and the difficult road ahead in finding forgiveness, both from others and themselves.

This chapter poignantly captures the theme of confronting the truth and the painful process of moving beyond illusions. It sets the stage for the characters' journey towards healing and self-discovery, highlighting the transformative power of facing one's realities.

THE GATHERING STORM

"The Gathering Storm," builds upon the escalating tensions and impending changes in the lives of the central characters. This chapter symbolizes the build-up of unresolved issues and emotions that are about to culminate in significant confrontations and decisions. The narrative opens with Mark, who is increasingly feeling the pressure of his professional and personal life converging into a storm he no longer feels capable of controlling. His once-stellar reputation in the business world begins to show cracks as whispers of his personal life start affecting his professional relationships. He feels the impending storm of potential career repercussions looming over him, adding to his already heavy burden of guilt and regret.

Simultaneously, Selina is facing her own gathering storm. The social circles she once navigated with ease are now fraught with whispers and judgmental glances. Her philanthropic work, which she had always taken pride in, now seems like a futile attempt to wash away the sins of her past. The tension within her own family, strained by the revelation of her affair and their criminal history, reaches a boiling point.

For Lerato, the gathering storm is one of emotional upheaval. She finds herself at a crossroads, torn between her love for Mark and the hurt his betrayal has caused. Her inner turmoil is compounded by external pressures from family and friends, each offering their advice and expectations on how she should proceed.

Selina's husband, meanwhile, is caught in a storm of legal and emotional complexities. The dissolution of their marriage brings forth a myriad of legal challenges, entangled with his own emotional struggle to reconcile with the reality of their broken relationship. As the chapter progresses, Mark and Selina, each in their respective lives, brace for the impact of the gathering storm. They are acutely aware that the choices they make in the face of these challenges will have far-reaching consequences.

The climax of the chapter occurs during a chance encounter between Mark and Selina at a mutual friend's event. This meeting serves as a catalyst for bringing their underlying tensions and unresolved emotions to the surface. The chapter ends with a sense of impending change, a realization that the storm they have been trying to stave off is about to break.

"The Gathering Storm" sets a tone of anticipation and foreboding, highlighting the inevitability of facing the consequences of one's actions. It prepares the ground for the upcoming chapters where the characters must confront the realities of their situations and make pivotal decisions.

REVELATIONS UNEARTHED

"Revelations Unearthed," focuses on the uncovering of critical truths and insights that significantly alter the perspectives and paths of the central characters. This chapter is key in bringing to light hidden aspects and leading to transformative changes in the narrative. The chapter begins with a surprising twist involving Mark. He receives unexpected information about his father's past that sheds new light on his family history and his own upbringing.

This revelation forces Mark to re-evaluate his perceptions of his father, the decisions he made in his youth, and how these elements influenced his own life choices. This newfound understanding presents Mark with a complex mix of emotions, as he grapples with a sense of empathy for his father intertwined with lingering feelings of resentment.

Selina, meanwhile, faces her own ground-breaking revelations. She uncovers truths about her family's past that were kept hidden from her, revealing a different side to her father's character and his actions. This discovery challenges her longstanding beliefs about her family and herself. It forces her to confront the notion that her life, which she believed was a rebellion against her family's legacy, may have been influenced by misconceptions and incomplete information.

Lerato, in her journey of self-discovery and healing, comes across a revelation about her own past that puts her relationship with Mark in a new light. This insight provides her with a deeper understanding of her own needs and desires, guiding her towards a path of self-empowerment and decision-making about her future.

Selina's husband also encounters revelations of his own, both about Selina and himself. His journey through the breakdown of their marriage leads him to uncover aspects of his personality and values that he had previously overlooked. This self-realization is pivotal in his process of moving forward and finding closure.

The chapter culminates in a dramatic scene where Mark and Selina meet, each armed with their new insights. Their conversation is transformative, as they share the revelations they have uncovered. This exchange leads to a deeper understanding between them, but also to the realization that their relationship, formed under the shadow of their misunderstood pasts, needs to be re-evaluated. "Revelations Unearthed" is rich in discovery and introspection, marking a turning point in the narrative. It explores the impact of newfound truths on the characters' understanding of themselves and their relationships, setting the stage for their subsequent actions and decisions in the evolving story.

BLOODLINES ENTWINED

"Bloodlines Entwined," goes into the intricate connections between the past and present, highlighting how the familial histories of Mark and Selina are more intertwined than they initially realized. This chapter brings to the forefront the theme of destiny versus choice, as the characters grapple with the implications of their entangled bloodlines.

The chapter begins with a stunning revelation that ties Mark and Selina's families together in an unexpected way. A chance discovery, perhaps a hidden letter or a confession from an older family member, reveals that their families have been connected for generations, their histories interwoven in ways that Mark and Selina had never imagined. This revelation sheds new light on their current situation, adding layers of complexity to their relationship and the choices they have made.

Mark, reeling from the discovery, begins to see his past in a new light. He reflects on how the actions of the previous generations have unwittingly shaped his life, influencing his decisions and his path. This realization prompts Mark to question the extent of his free will and the role of destiny in his life.

Selina, equally affected by the revelation, starts to piece together the puzzle of her own family history.

She understands that the legacy she has been trying to escape is more deeply rooted than she thought. This understanding forces Selina to confront her feelings of responsibility towards her family legacy and her desire to forge her own path.

The narrative then weaves through the perspectives of Lerato and Selina's husband, exploring how this revelation impacts their views on their respective situations. Lerato finds herself contemplating the idea of fate and questioning whether her relationship with Mark was ever meant to be. Selina's husband, dealing with the aftermath of their marriage, begins to see the broader picture of Selina's struggles and the historical forces that have influenced their lives.

As the chapter progresses, Mark and Selina meet to discuss the implications of their intertwined bloodlines. Their conversation is charged with a mix of shock, understanding, and a sense of inevitability. They ponder the possibility that their coming together was more than mere coincidence, perhaps a convergence of their families' entangled histories.

"Bloodlines Entwined" concludes with both characters in a state of introspection, contemplating the roles of fate and choice in their lives. The chapter ends on an ambiguous note, leaving the reader to wonder how Mark and Selina will navigate this newfound understanding of their shared past and what decisions they will make about their intertwined futures.

This chapter deepens the narrative by exploring the theme of intergenerational connections and the lasting impact of family legacies. It sets the stage for the characters to confront the intricate web of their pasts and decide how to move forward in light of these revelations.

FACES OF THE ENEMY

"Faces of the Enemy," brings the underlying tensions and conflicts to a head, as Mark and Selina, along with their families, confront the realities of their intertwined histories and the present conflicts. This chapter highlights the complexities of relationships and the blurred lines between love, hatred, and understanding.

The chapter opens with a dramatic scene where members of both Mark and Selina's families come face to face, perhaps at a legal proceeding or a mediation session. This encounter, charged with emotions, brings together the people who have been indirectly affected by Mark and Selina's affair and their families' past actions. The meeting is tense, with accusations and grievances aired, and the pain and anger that have been simmering beneath the surface finally erupting.

During this confrontation, Mark and Selina are forced to face the pain they have caused not just to each other and their spouses, but also to their extended families. They are confronted with the 'faces of their enemies,' but these faces are not just those of outsiders — they are also family members, loved ones, people they once trusted.

This chapter also explores the theme of 'enemy' in a more introspective way. Mark and Selina each grapple with the realization that the greatest enemy can often be oneself — their own choices, actions, and the parts of themselves they have struggled with. They are forced to confront the fact that their affair was not just an escape from their marriages, but also a manifestation of their struggles with their personal demons and family legacies.

Lerato and Selina's husband, integral to this chapter, face their own battles. Lerato finds herself confronting her feelings of betrayal and her notions of justice and forgiveness. Selina's husband grapples with his understanding of loyalty and betrayal, and whether his perception of Selina has been clouded by his own biases and the revelations about her family.

The chapter culminates in a moment of unexpected understanding and empathy among the characters. In the face of shared pain and complicated histories, there is a moment where they see beyond their anger and grievances, recognizing the shared humanity in each other. This does not resolve the conflicts but adds a layer of complexity to how they perceive each other and their situations.

"Faces of the Enemy" concludes with Mark and Selina reflecting on the day's events, each contemplating the next steps in their personal journeys. The chapter ends with a sense of unresolved tension, as the characters are left to ponder the intricate web of relationships and the path to reconciliation or closure.

This chapter deepens the emotional landscape of the story, highlighting the multi-faceted nature of conflict and the difficulty of navigating familial and personal relationships in the wake of deep betrayal and historical burdens. It sets a tone of introspection and tentative understanding, paving the way for the characters' ultimate resolutions.

A TRUTH TOO HEAVY

"A Truth Too Heavy," captures the emotional weight and complexity of the truths that have surfaced, focusing on how the characters deal with these revelations and the heavy burden they impose on their lives and decisions. The chapter begins with Mark in a state of deep contemplation. The recent revelations about his and Selina's intertwined family histories, combined with the fallout of their affair, weigh heavily on him. He grapples with the enormity of the situation, feeling overwhelmed by the cascade of truths that have come to light. These truths are not just about his family's past, but also about himself, his actions, and the impact they have had on those he cares about.

Selina, similarly, finds herself burdened by the weight of the truth. The realization that her life has been shaped by a history she only partially understood leaves her feeling lost. She reflects on the choices she has made, questioning whether they were ever truly her own or if they were influenced by a legacy she never fully grasped.

Lerato, facing her own set of heavy truths, begins to process the reality of her broken marriage and the man she thought she knew. The knowledge that Mark's betrayal was not just a momentary lapse, but part of a deeper pattern tied to his past, forces her to reassess her life and her future.

Selina's husband is also confronted with a truth too heavy to bear – the understanding that the woman he loved and the life they built together were based on omissions and falsehoods. This realization challenges him to rethink his own identity and what he wants from life moving forward.

As the chapter unfolds, Mark and Selina meet in a moment of shared vulnerability. They talk openly about the weight of their truths, the guilt they carry, and the uncertainty of their futures. This conversation is a cathartic one, marked by a sense of resignation and a faint hope for redemption. The chapter also touches on the broader implications of these truths on the families of Mark and Selina. The families are forced to confront their own roles in the perpetuation of certain patterns and secrets, leading to a collective reckoning with the past.

"A Truth Too Heavy" concludes with each character coming to terms with the fact that some truths change everything, leaving indelible marks on their lives. The chapter ends on a sober note, with each character reflecting on the path forward in the wake of these heavy revelations.

This chapter delves into the emotional and psychological impact of facing difficult truths, exploring themes of responsibility, self-awareness, and the potential for growth and healing. It sets the stage for the final resolutions in the story, highlighting the transformative power of truth, no matter how heavy.

EPILOGUE: SILENCE OF THE FALLEN

"Epilogue: Silence of the Fallen," serves as a reflective conclusion to the tumultuous journey of the characters. It encapsulates the aftermath of their decisions, the lessons learned, and the quiet that follows the resolution of their conflicts. As the dust settles on the events that have unfolded, Mark, Selina, Lerato, and Selina's husband each find themselves in a state of introspection. The epilogue paints a picture of their lives after the storm has passed, highlighting the changes they have undergone and the futures they face.

Mark, having come to terms with his past and the consequences of his actions, starts a new chapter in his life. He engages in work that is more meaningful to him, focusing on rebuilding his sense of self and his integrity. The lessons he has learned from his affair with Selina and the revelations about his family guide him in his quest for a more authentic and grounded existence.

Selina, similarly, emerges from the experience transformed. The breakdown of her marriage and the confronting of her family's history have prompted a deep personal growth. She dedicates herself to causes that genuinely resonate with her, stepping out of the shadow of her family's legacy. Selina finds solace in helping others, using her experiences to guide and support those facing similar challenges.

Lerato, now divorced from Mark, finds strength in her independence. She rediscovers passions and interests that she had put aside, and her journey becomes one of self-discovery and empowerment. Lerato's resilience and newfound confidence shine through, serving as an inspiration to those around her.

Selina's husband embarks on his path of healing and understanding. He learns to forgive and to let go of the past, focusing on building a future that is true to his values and aspirations. His journey is marked by a quiet determination and a newfound appreciation for honesty and authenticity in relationships.

The epilogue also touches on the quieter, more reflective moments of the characters. They each find moments of peace and understanding, a silence that is not empty but full of the lessons learned and the wisdom gained. It's a silence that speaks of resilience, of the capacity to rise from the ashes of fallen dreams and to rebuild.

"Epilogue: Silence of the Fallen" concludes the book with a sense of closure and hope. The characters' journeys, marked by pain and struggle, end with a quiet acknowledgment of their strength and the possibility of new beginnings. This epilogue serves as a testament to the enduring human spirit and the capacity for growth and transformation in the face of adversity. It leaves the reader with a sense of resolution and the understanding that even in silence, there is a profound strength and a whisper of continuing life.

AFTERWORD

As I close the final chapter of this story, I am compelled to reflect on the journey that led to the creation of **Secret Lives, Hidden Truths.** This narrative, woven with themes of love, betrayal, and redemption, was born from a desire to explore the complexities of human relationships and the shadows cast by our pasts.

The characters of Mark, Selina, Lerato, and Selina's husband were conceived as embodiments of our struggles with personal demons, societal expectations, and the burdens of family legacies. Their stories, though fictional, mirror the conflicts and challenges that many of us face in our quest for authenticity and fulfilment.

The process of writing this book was one of introspection and discovery. I delved into the intricacies of human emotions, the tangled webs we weave with our choices, and the resilience required to face the consequences of those choices. The journey of each character is a testament to the human capacity for growth, forgiveness, and the relentless pursuit of redemption.

I would like to extend my heartfelt gratitude to those who supported me throughout the writing process. To my editor, for their keen insights and unwavering patience; to my family and friends, for their encouragement and honest feedback; and to you, the readers, for embarking on this journey with me.

As you reflect on the story of Mark, Selina, and their families, I hope it resonates with you, provokes thought, and perhaps offers a new perspective on the choices we make and the paths we tread.

Thank you for being a part of this journey.